Rookie Year!

Art: Alan Evans
Story: Alan Evans and Justin Riley
Color Assists: Aaron Daly
Chapter 14 Cover: Keith Malkowski
Rival Angels created by
Alan Evans

www.RivalAngels.com

Rival Angels Season 2, Volume 2. ISBN 978-0-9827013-5-5.
Rival Angels and all associated characters and their distinct likenesses are © 2016 of Alan Evans. The events presented in this book are entirely fictional. Any similarity to persons living or dead is purely coincidental. No portion of this comic book may be reproduced by any means (digital or print) without express permission, except for purposes of review.

RIVAL ANGELS

CHAPTER 7

"AND THAT IS HOW CHANGE HAPPENS. ONE GESTURE. ONE PERSON. ONE MOMENT AT A TIME."
-LIBBA BRAY

SUNDAY EVENING AT THE **ANGEL DOME**, IN CHICAGO.

'Armageddon Annihilation' Pay-per-view

JEFF, WHAT A NIGHT IT'S BEEN!

WE'VE HAD SOME *OUTSTANDING* MATCHES TONIGHT, *DAWN*.

THE *CATGIRLS* PULLED THEIR USUAL SHENANIGANS TO EDGE OUT, *TOO HOTT*!

LORETTA AND *SARA* JUST WEREN'T HOT ENOUGH.

DAMAGE INC. STARTED OFF STRONG WITH *KYRA GOLD* DEFEATING *JENNIFER NEEDLES*.

DAMAGE INC. OVER HELL'S BELLES!

THE FORMER TV CHAMP, *KAT SMITH*, WAS BACK TO HER WINNING WAYS AGAINST *NIKKI FOXX*.

HELL'S BELLES OVER DAMAGE INC.!

VICTORIA SHOWED RIDICULOUS STRENGTH AND GUTS IN HER VICTORY TONIGHT OVER *RAMPAGE*.

ADMIT IT, DAWN! YOU DIDN'T THINK THE 'LIL DRAGON' COULD PULL IT OFF!

SUN WONG IS A FORMER CHAMPION AND NEVER TO BE TAKEN LIGHTLY.

I WILL ADMIT THAT I THOUGHT THE ODDS WERE IN *XTINA'S* FAVOR.

THIS ISN'T 'HUNGER GAMES,' DAWN!

YOU SEEM TO BE WELL-VERSED IN THAT SERIES.

SUN WOULD'VE BEAT *KATNISS* WITH HER OWN BOW AND ATOMIC FISSION'D *PETA* AND *GAYLE* BACK TO DISTRICT 12.

I READ STUFF.

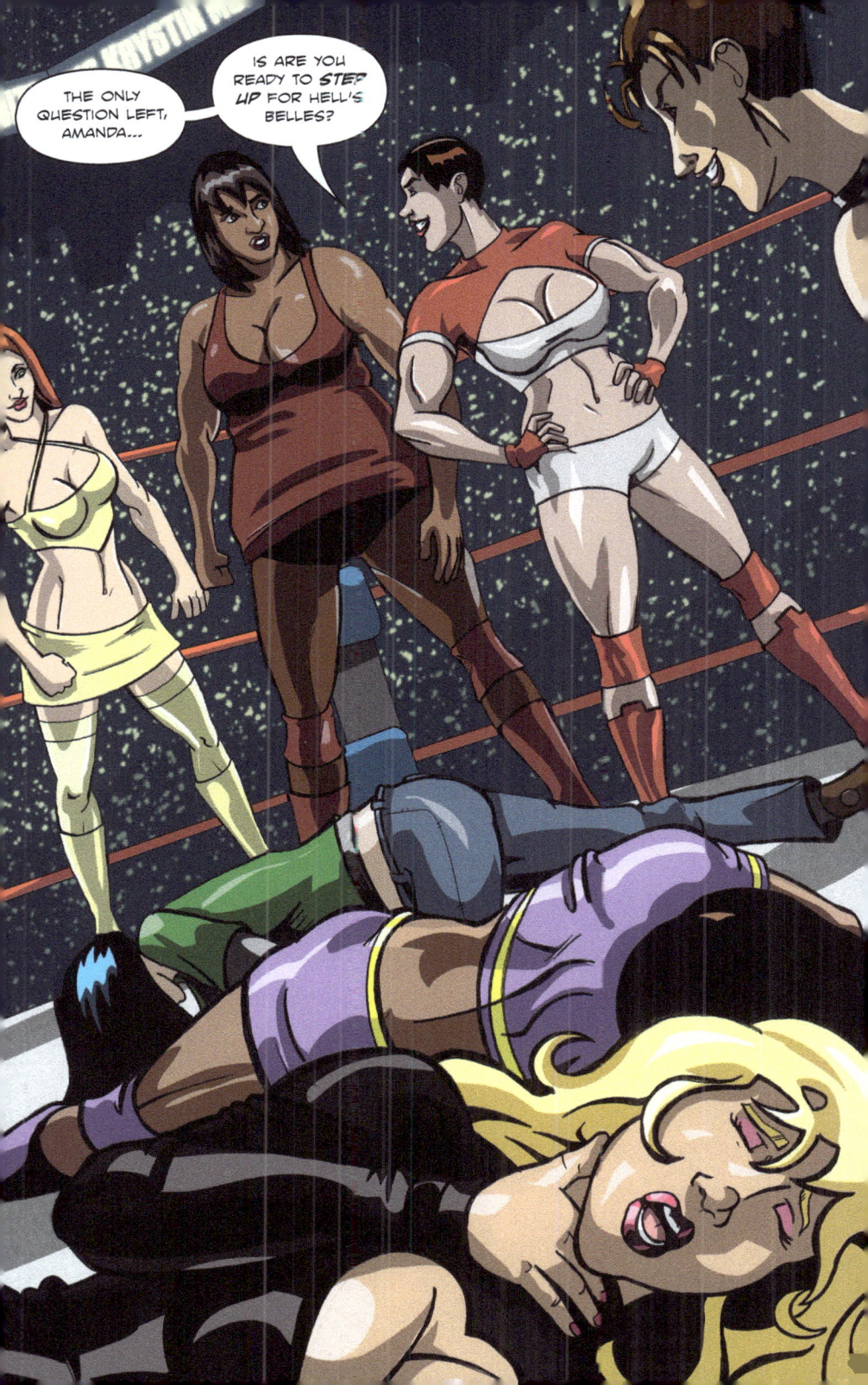

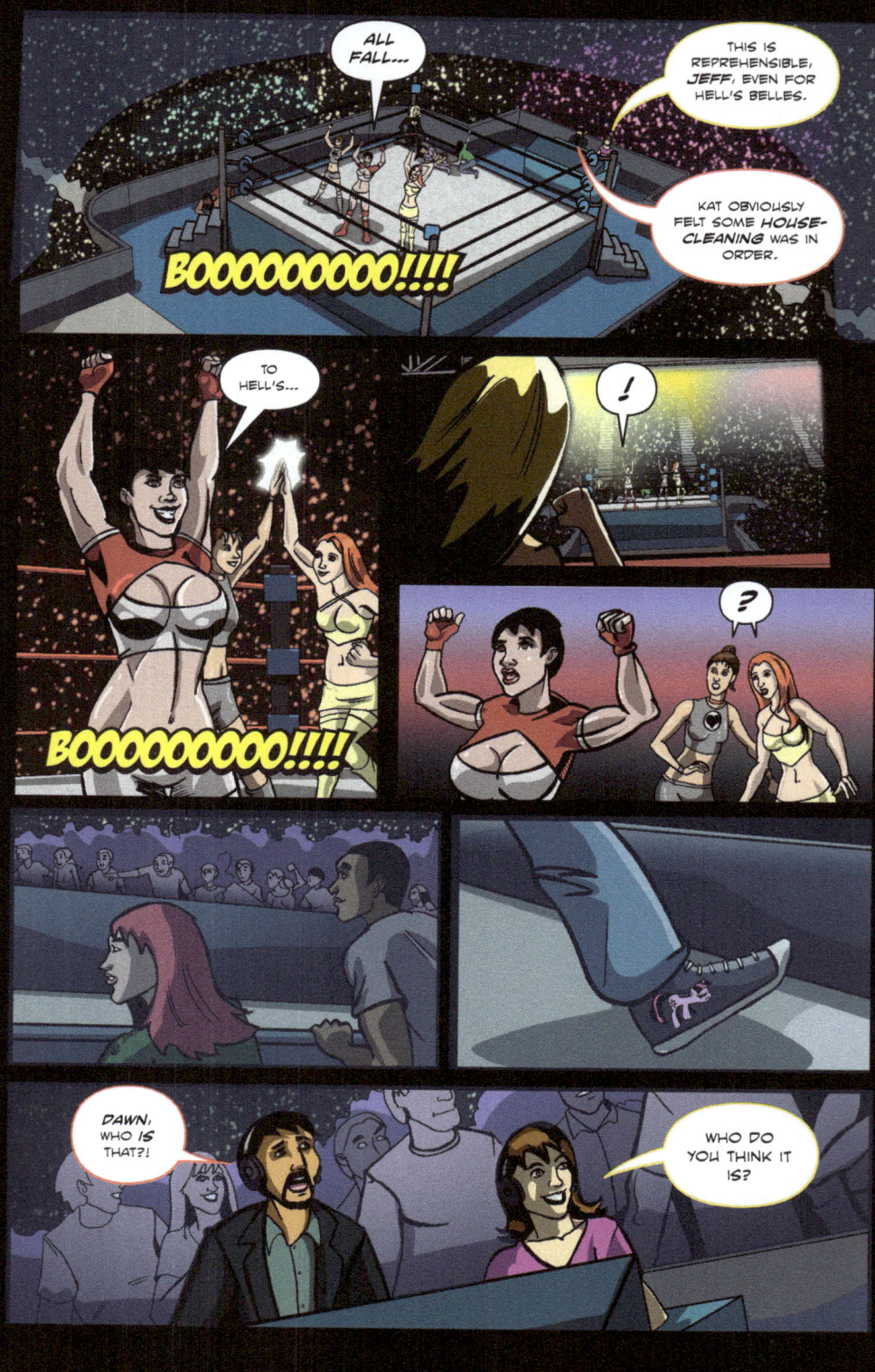

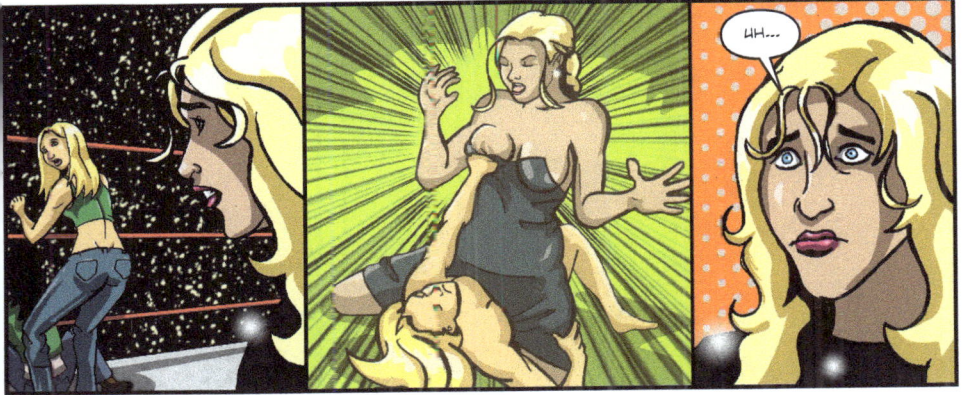

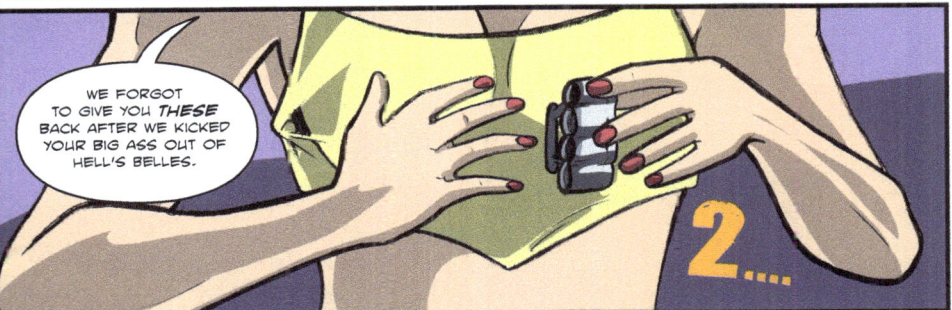
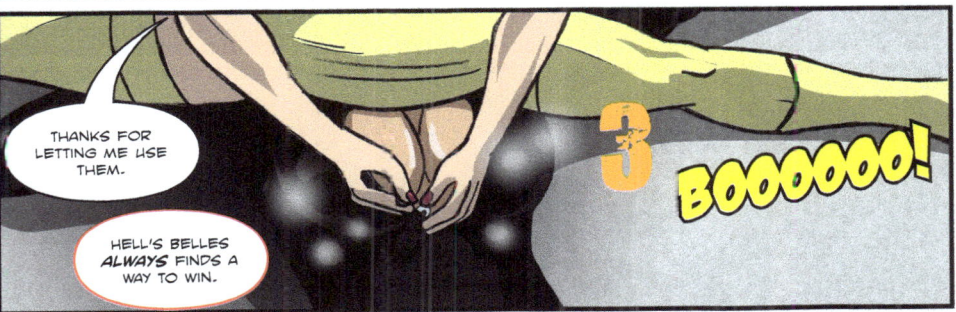

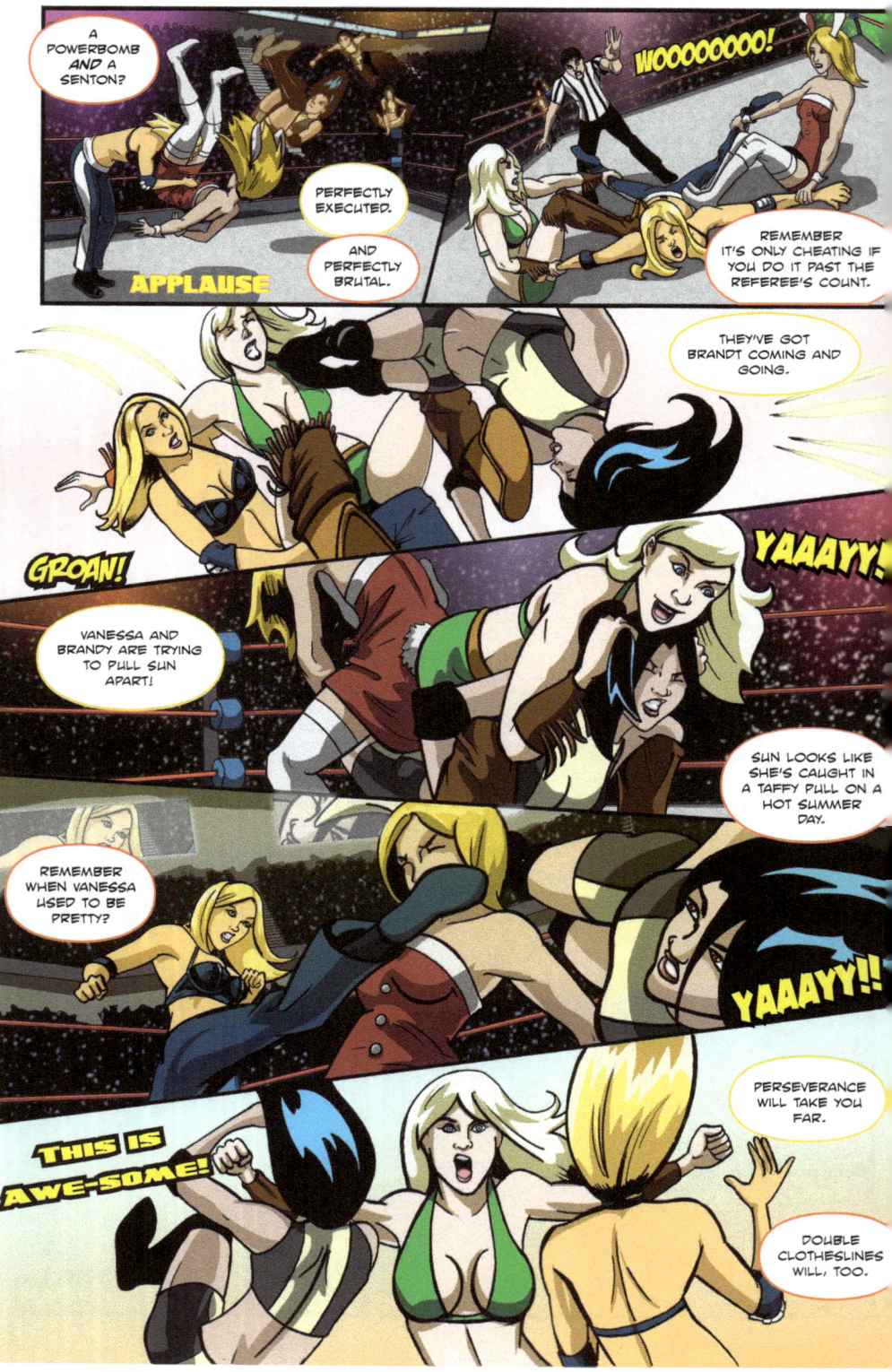

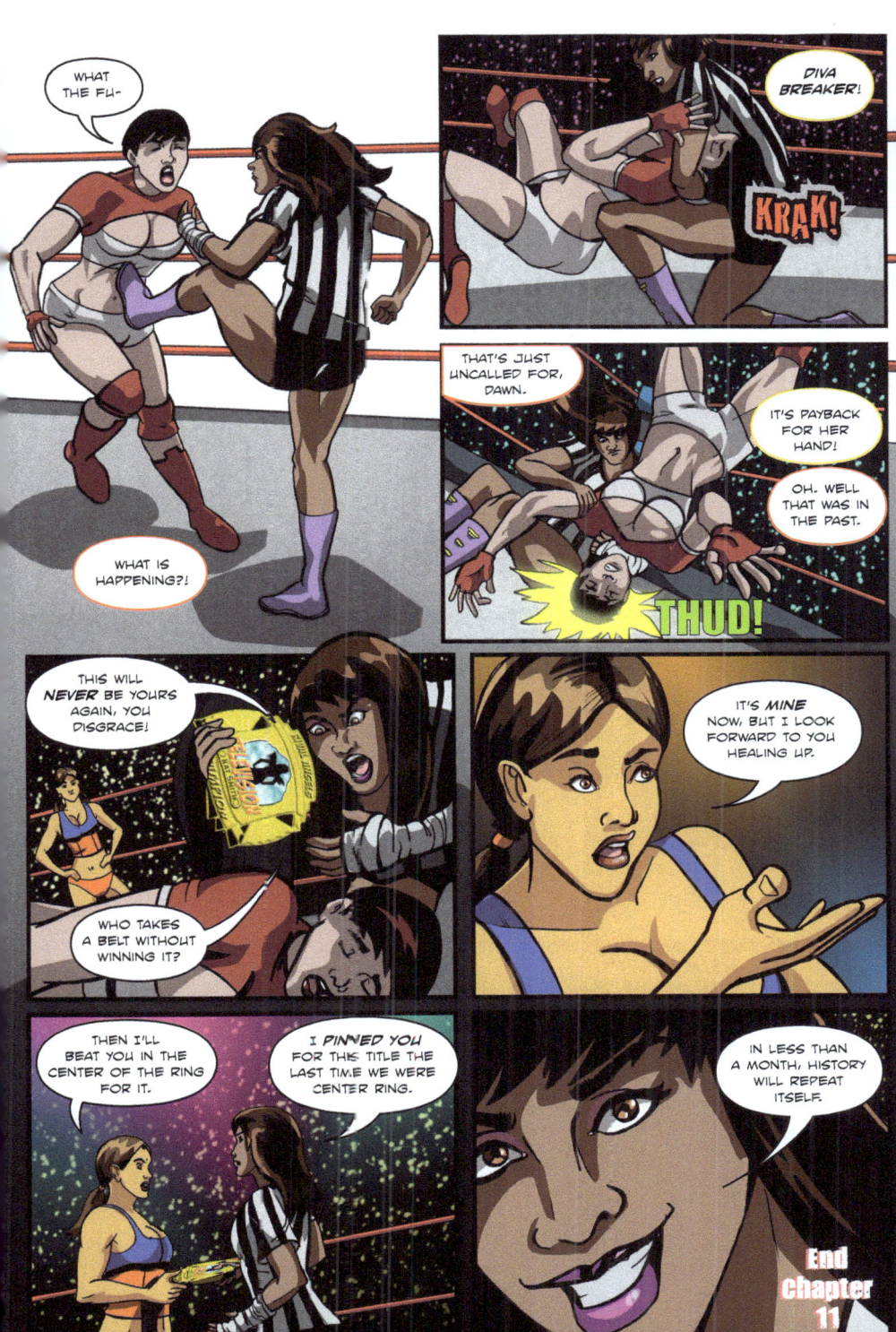

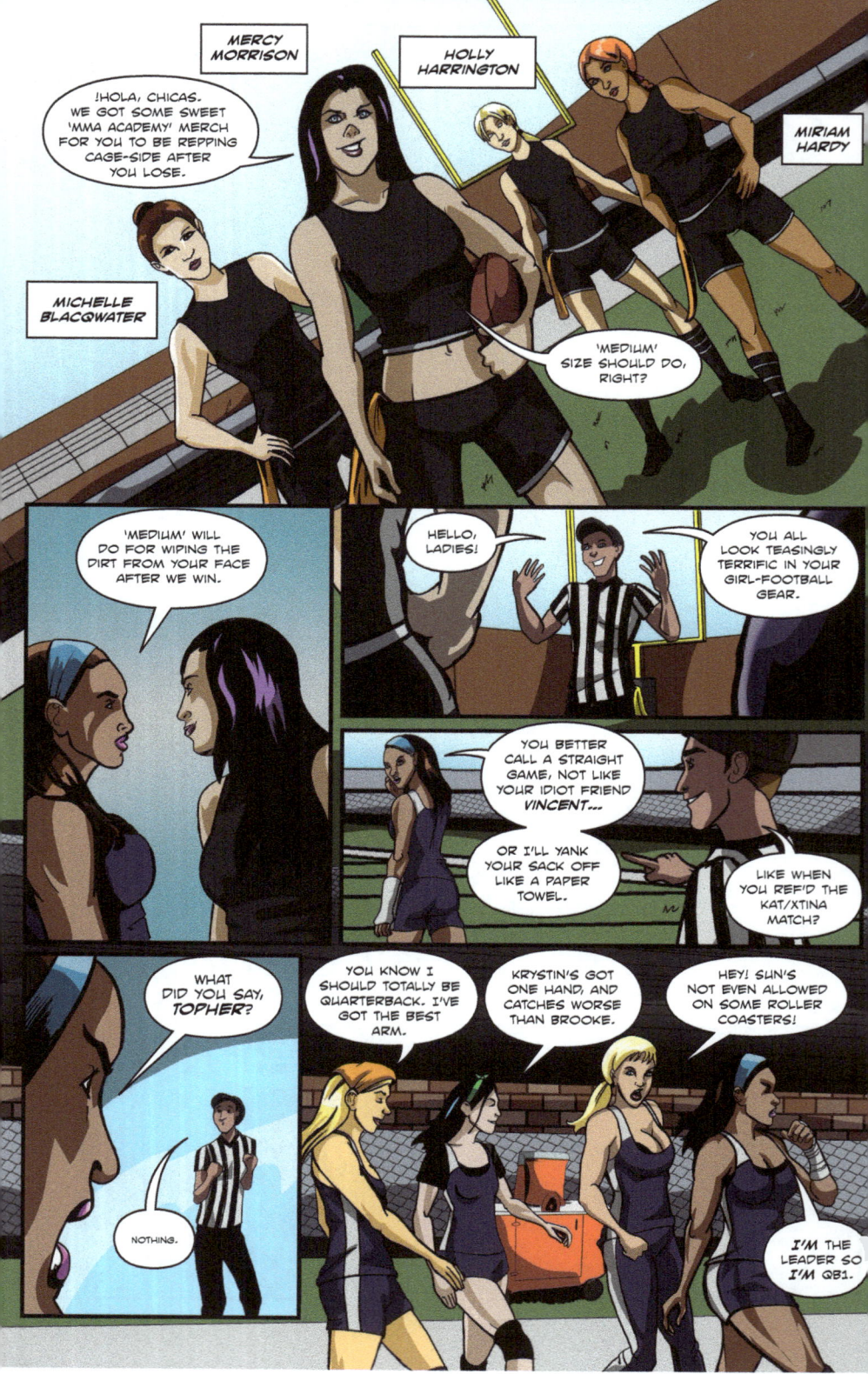

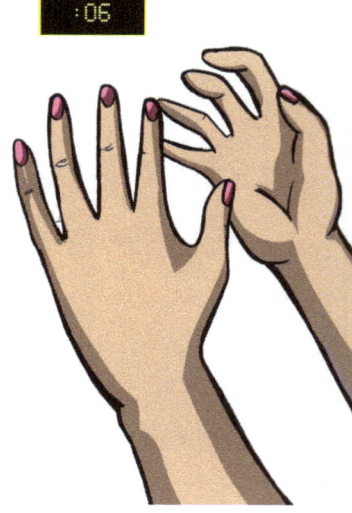

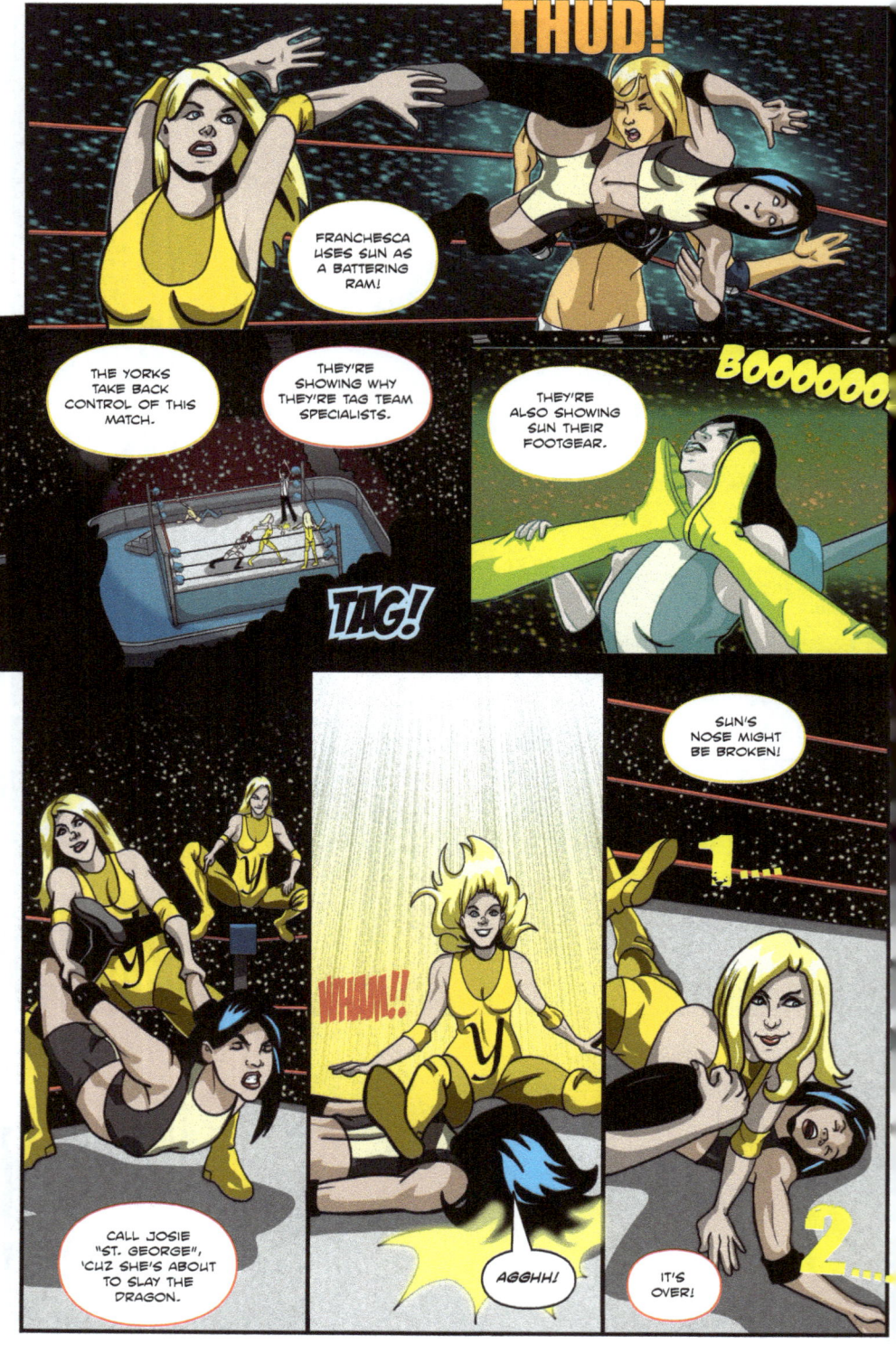

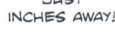

End chapter 13

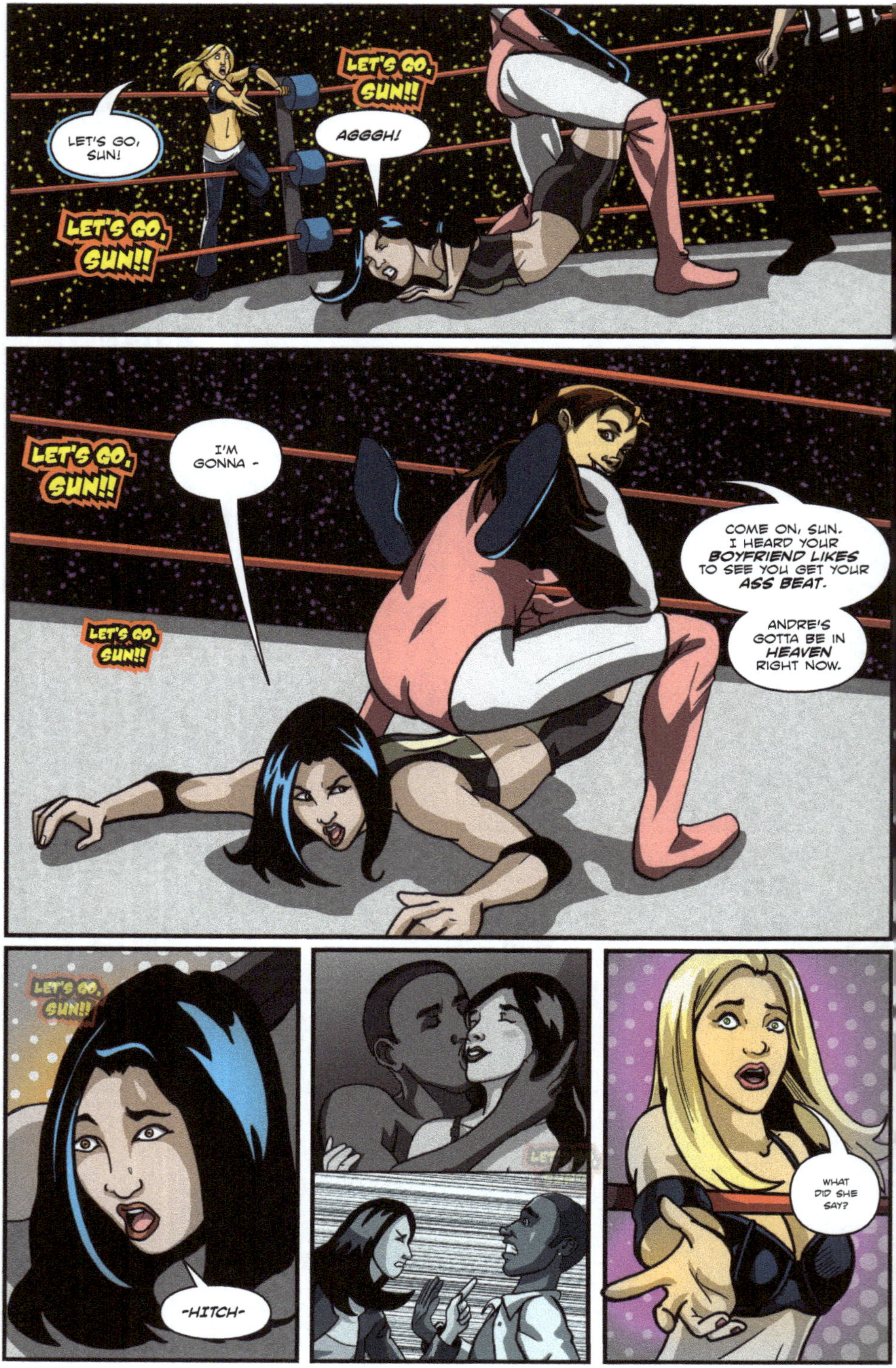

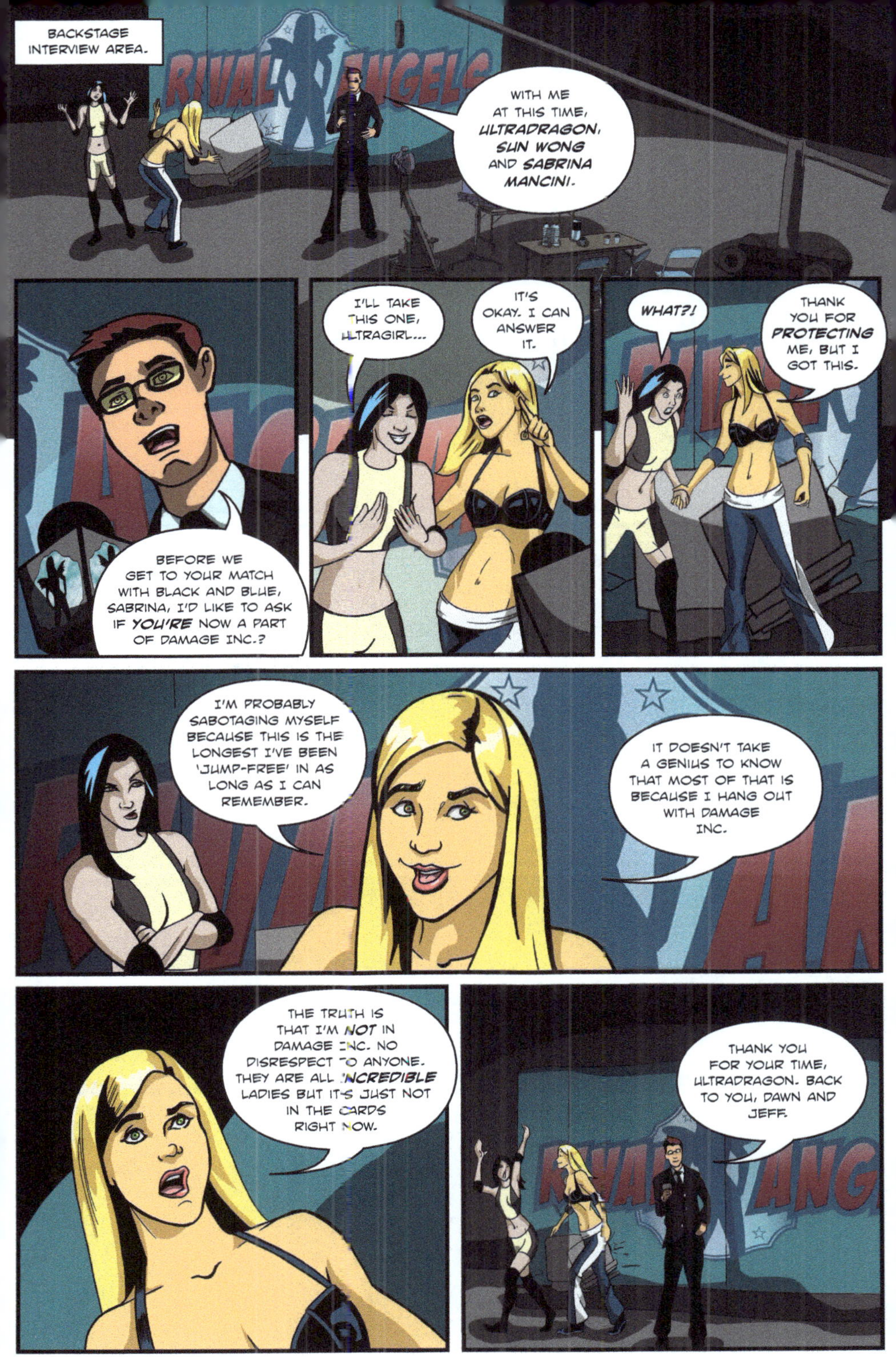

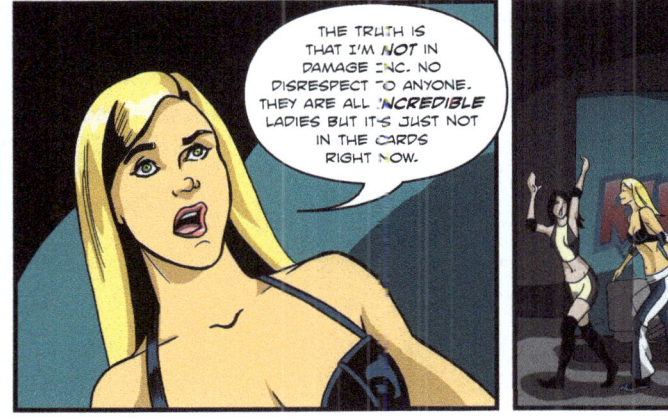

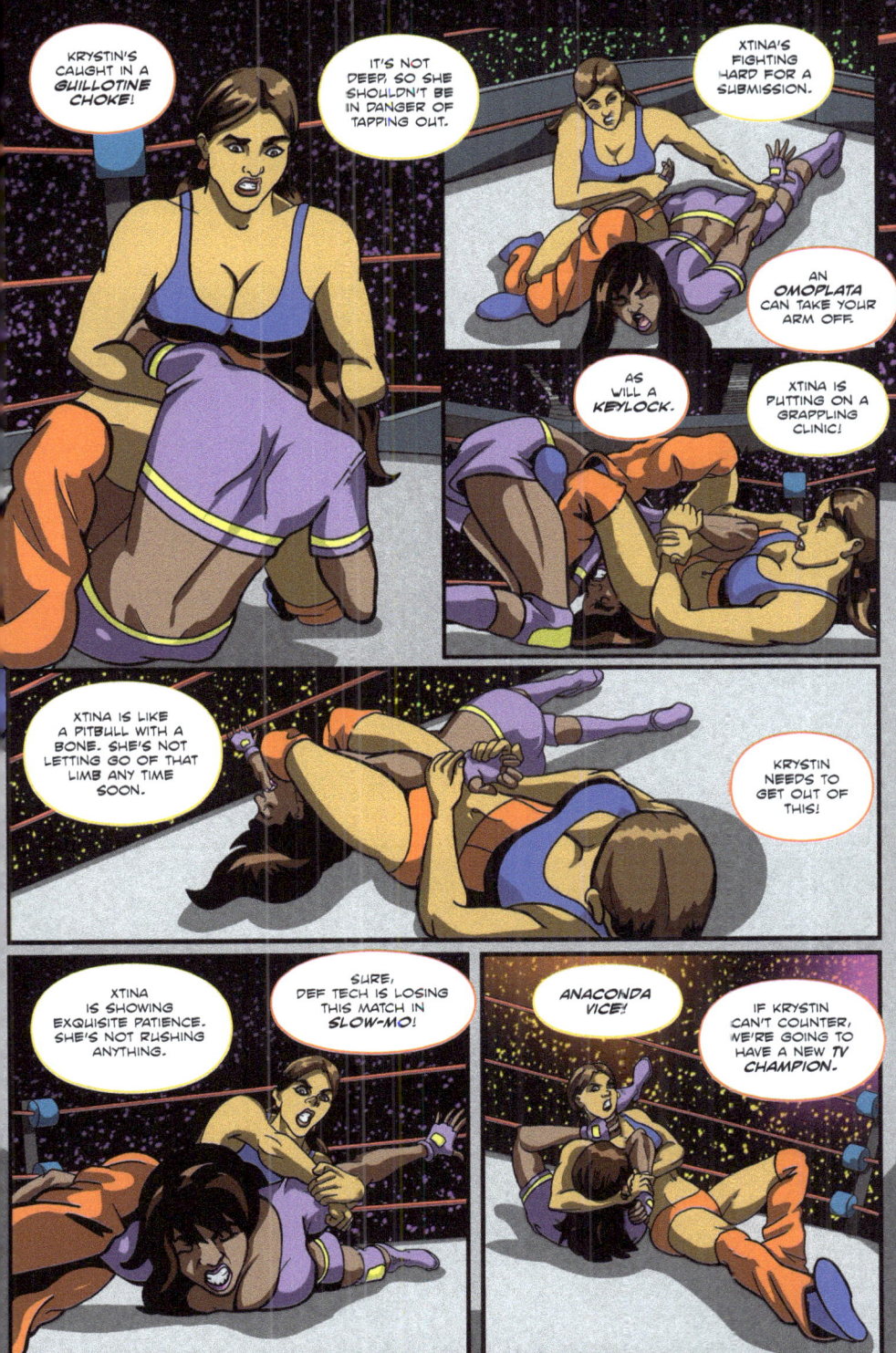

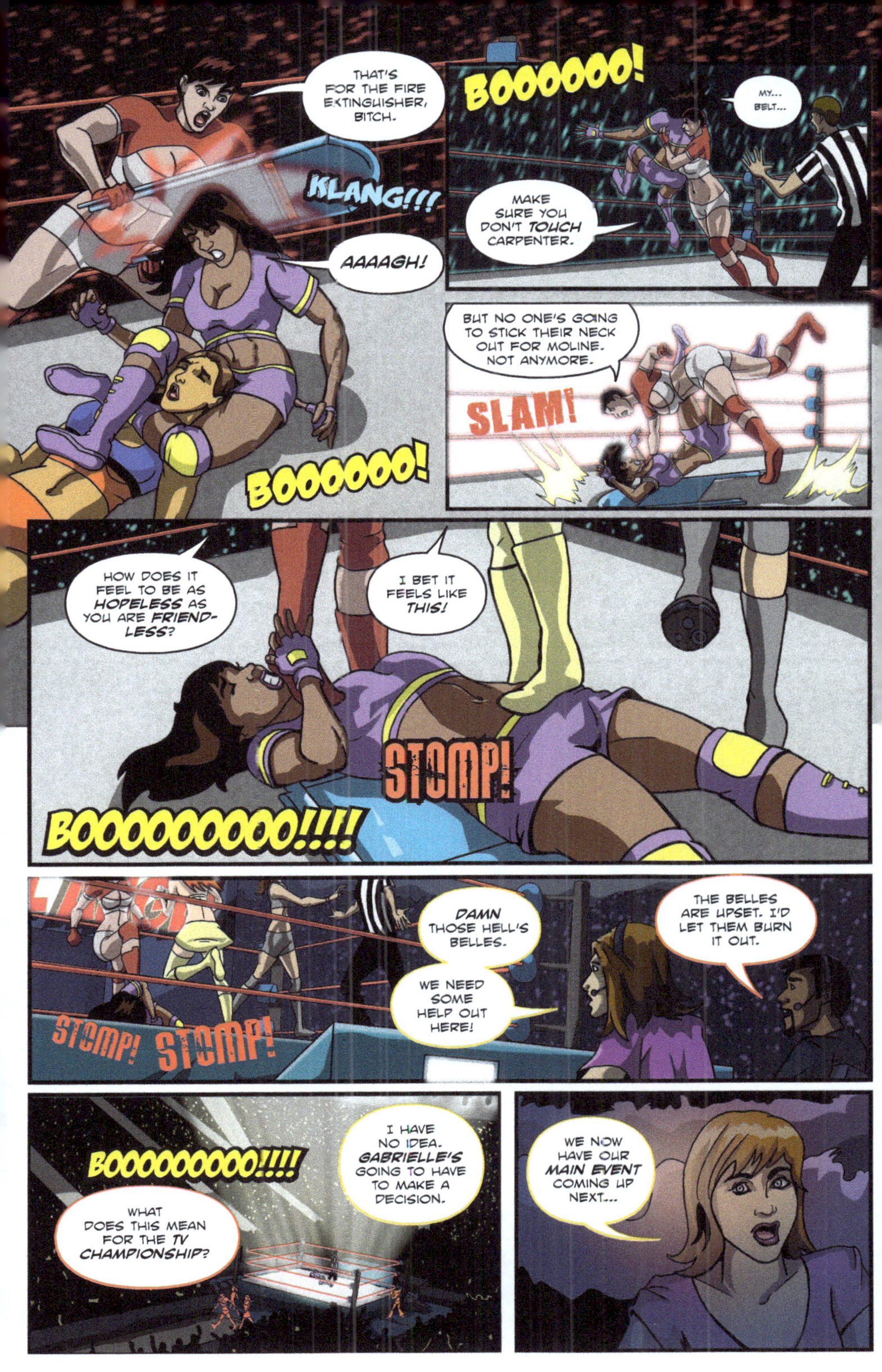

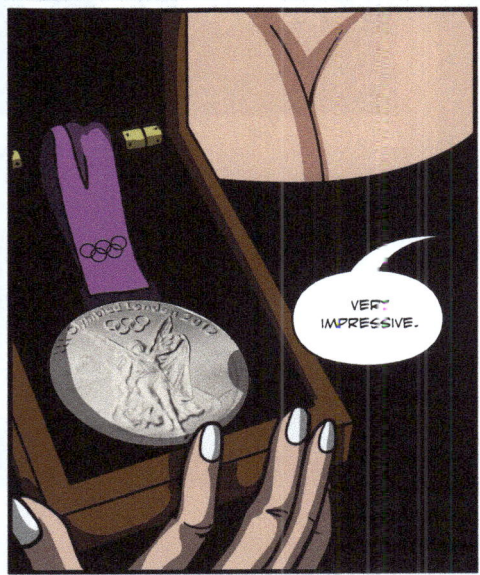

NEXT IN RIVAL ANGELS SEASON 3

Acknowledgements

Special thanks to the Rival Angels readers!

Kickstarter Sponsors and Patrons

Jim Payne
MAYYDAY
Brian Bishop
Stoney
Peter Migala
Travis Clemens
James Carey
Saikyodragon
Jay Magnum
Bob Pullano

Ring Crew

To those that listen,
indulge, build up and support.

Aaron
Danny
Keith
Lora
Justin
Tracie

www.ingramcontent.com/pod-product-compliance
Ingram Content Group UK Ltd.
Pitfield, Milton Keynes, MK11 3LW, UK
UKHW021256180426
11947UKWH00011B/804